Justin's Tea Party

Karen Clark
Illustrated by Jamie Charles

Copyright © 2023 by Karen Clark. All rights reserved.
This book may not be reproduced or stored in whole or in part
by any means without the written permission of the author
except for brief quotations for the purpose of review.

ISBN: 978-1-960146-75-5 (hard cover)
978-1-960146-76-2 (soft cover)

Edited by: Amy Ashby

Published by Warren Publishing
Charlotte, NC
www.warrenpublishing.net
Printed in the United States

For my nieces and nephews, who inspired me.
To D, C, S, & J—Thank you for always supporting and loving me.
I love you more than I can ever express.
To Jamie—Thank you for making this come alive.

"I'm going to Hannah's house for the tea party!" Lily called to her mom as she ran out the back door.
Justin sat glumly at the kitchen table, watching her go. He liked tea and wanted to go to the party too.

Hannah had a tea party every Friday. Justin had tried to go once; he dressed in his best shirt and walked over with Lily.
But Hannah said, "Tea parties aren't for boys."

So one day, Justin decided to have his own tea party. Having never hosted one before, he invited his dinosaur Spike, his bear Amos, and his knight Sir Cooper the Great to a practice party.

Justin's mom made tea and cookies and cut up some fruit too. Everyone sat outside at the patio table. Justin poured tea and passed out the cookies and some fruit to each of his guests.

Everyone was very polite and said, "Thank you." Then, everything started to go wrong ....

Amos didn't like tea and made a face that looked like he had eaten a worm. Spike, however, loved his tea so much that he gulped it down all at once with a long *Slurp!* Of course, that resulted in an earsplitting *Burp!*

Sir Cooper thought this was very rude and poked Spike with his sword.
"Hey! Say excuse me!" he said.
"Why should I?" asked Spike, and he threw a strawberry at Sir Cooper.
Fortunately, Justin saw it and caught the strawberry before it landed. *Splat!* Justin's hand was now all red and sticky.
"Stop!" cried Justin.

His guests looked at him. They could tell Justin was upset, so they got quiet.
"Sir Cooper, apologize to Spike," Justin said.
"I'm sorry I poked you," said Sir Cooper.
"And I'm sorry I didn't say 'excuse me,'" said Spike.

The party continued.

Sir Cooper attempted to tell a silly story. "One time I hunted a dragon that smelled like dirty socks—" he started, but Justin stopped him.

"Tea parties are fancy and serious," he said. "You aren't supposed to be silly."

Sir Cooper frowned.

After eating the cookies, Amos was so thirsty. "Can I have something else to drink?" he asked.

"But this is a tea party," Justin said. "You have to drink tea."

Amos started to cry, and he dumped his tea onto the table. Some of the tea splashed onto his fruit and that made him cry harder. Tears streamed down his face, making plopping noises on the table.

Spike started to laugh, but he realized his rudeness when Sir Cooper brandished his sword.

"Don't cry, Amos," said Sir Cooper as he tried to comfort his friend.

But when Amos saw Sir Cooper's sword, he thought Sir Cooper was angry with him. Amos began to cry so hard, he fell off his chair with a tremendous crash!

Spike couldn't hold back his laughter anymore. "He he he!" he cried and spat his tea across the table, where it hit Justin right in the face. *Sploosh!*

Poor Justin! He didn't know what to do. He was wet, one guest was crying, and his tea party was a wreck.
"This is all wrong!" Justin cried. "A tea party isn't supposed to be like this. Don't you know how to act at a tea party?"

He got up and went to the kitchen, leaving his guests outside.
"What happened?" his mom asked, seeing the mess.
Justin explained everything that had gone wrong.

"Why does it have to be a fancy tea party, Justin? Is that what you wanted?"
"Well, aren't tea parties supposed to be fancy and serious?" Justin replied.
"Oh, my dear," she said. "It's your party. It can be whatever you want it to be."

So, Justin went back outside and tried again. This time, things were much better. No one cried or threatened anyone, and Justin let go of his rules a little.
Then Justin thought about what his mom had said.

The next Friday, he invited his two best friends, Samuel and Shiloh. Samuel brought his favorite monster truck, and Shiloh brought a tiger named Stripes.

Everything was set up just like Justin's practice party, but this time Justin was ready. After he poured the tea and passed out plates of cookies and fruit, he told a silly story. Everyone laughed!

When Shiloh tried the tea and did not like it, Justin said, "Here, try it with some milk and honey."

When Shiloh *still* did not like it, Justin said, "That's okay. You don't have to like the same things I like. Do you like lemonade?"

"Is it okay if I don't eat any strawberries?" Samuel asked.
"Oh, I can eat them for you. I love strawberries," said Shiloh.

The boys each ate and drank what they liked and ate all the cookies and fruit. Then they ran into the yard and played a game.

They were loud and silly, and they had such a great time that they did it again the next Friday.

And the next.

Justin's sister Lily asked if she could join.

Then other boys and girls from the neighborhood joined in too.

One afternoon, Justin knocked on Hannah's door. "Would you like to come to my house for tea tomorrow?" he asked her.

Hannah looked surprised. Then, she slowly uncrossed her arms, smiled, and said, "Yes, but only if you come to my house for tea next week."

Soon there were two tea parties—a silly one at Justin's house ...

and a fancy one at Hannah's house—and that suited everyone just fine.

It turned out Justin's mom had been right:
tea parties can be whatever you want them to be.

Printed in the USA
CPSIA information can be obtained
at www.ICGtesting.com
LVHW061749191023
761394LV00004B/40